THIS WALKER BOOK BELONGS TO:

_____

_____

_____

_____

For Kate

First published 1985 by Walker Books Ltd
87 Vauxhall Walk, London SE11 5HJ

This edition published 1988

2 4 6 8 10 9 7 5 3

© 1985 Jan Ormerod

This book has been typeset in Monotype Baskerville.

Printed in Italy.

British Library Cataloguing in Publication Data
A catalogue record for this book is
available from the British Library.

ISBN 0-7445-0929-7

Messy baby

Jan Ormerod

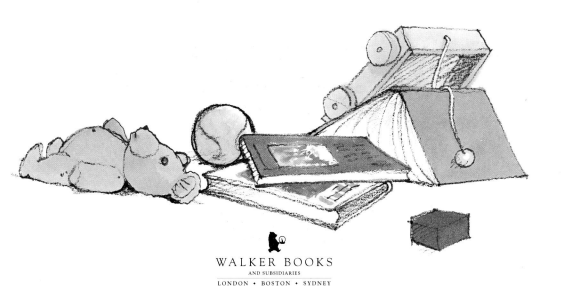

WALKER BOOKS
AND SUBSIDIARIES
LONDON • BOSTON • SYDNEY

Dad says,
    'Soft toys in the box.'

He says,
    'Books on the shelf.'

He says,
'Clothes in the cupboard.'

Dad says,
  'Bricks in the cart.'

He says,
    'Rubbish in the basket.'

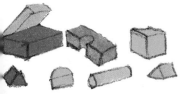

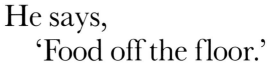

He says,
    'Food off the floor.'

'Oh no, what a mess!
   Oh, you messy baby!'

'Never mind,' Dad says.
'Let's start again.'